homonyms   (hom' ō nims)

words that look or sound the same, but have different meanings.

This story was written especially for

Lauren Greve

Merry Christmas! From,
Mommy and Daddy

December 25, 1993

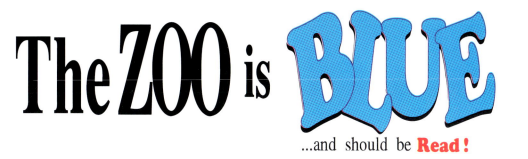

The ZOO is BLUE

...and should be **Read!**

An Outrageous Story Containing Over 20 Homonyms

By James W. Dixon

Lauren Greve
is the star of this story.

EXTRA   EXTRA

The Plain Dealer

Lauren Greve
PLANS A TRIP TO THE ZOO

Meghan, Clare, and Jessie plan to go along...

Even though going to the zoo can be a lot of fun, it's much more fun when you go with other people. That's why this trip promises to be such a grand success. Everyone knows how exciting it can be when there are more and more people involved. The word is out that this could just possibly be the biggest event of the season . . . it has also been reported that a certain special bag might be taken along . . . just in case . . . we don't have details on this rumor, however, we feel that it would be a pretty good idea to have something like that on hand. One never knows when one might need a bag of special things. We will bring you more of this story as your turn through the pages.

Animals Await Arrival

All the animals at the zoo are quite excited about the plans to be seen by the oncoming children. Some of them have been reported to have taken baths and combed their hair in anticipation of the arrival.

Weather

Sunny and clear . . . You couldn't ask for a better zoo day.

Mayor wants to go too . . .

Unfortunately, the mayor's busy schedule will not allow for a fun packed adventure to the zoo with the wonderful children. Says, "Maybe next time."

There's big news today...
This is the day for a Zoo Adventure!

They packed a tasty lunch with a pair of pear pies,
and a pudding cake. What a wonderful time
this was going to be!

CALENDAR

December 1993

25

Saturday

Lauren's bag

Lauren prepared a special bag for
the trip ... just in case.

8

Away they went. The children read a book and played with a big red ball in the car. Everyone was having a ball as they traveled to the zoo.

But, when they reached the main gate, they could see that something was very wrong. The zookeeper came running toward them with a gait so fast he ran out of his shoe!

Then his pocket watch fell out of his long coat, and a scraggly old monkey grabbed it and ran off. He longed to get it back, but the poor zookeeper was just too upset.

Everyone in the zoo was feeling blue.
Now who would coat the zoo in blue?

"I'm so blue... The zoo is blue. I don't know what to do!" he cried. Before they could ask him what he meant, he turned right and blew right past them. "The zoo is blue!" he cried again. No one understood this, so it seemed right to go inside and look for themselves.

Upon entering, they saw the zoo was indeed as blue as the zookeeper said. They went to the zebra corral where they were met by a glum looking creature with no stripes and a big blue tear in his eye. "We're blue because we have no stripes. We don't know what to do!" he cried.

This wouldn't do at all. Zebras are supposed to have stripes and that's all there is to it!

So Lauren reached into her bag and found a big black crayon.

In just a few minutes, stripes had been placed on every zebra in the place. And, even though some stripes were a little crooked, the zebras were happy again. They jumped and kicked and sang a zebra song!

Suddenly, everyone heard a faint sound. They thought they would faint when they saw a rhino standing in his clover. He had no horn and two blue tears running down his cheeks.

"I'm blue because I have no horn and I don't know what to do!" he cried.

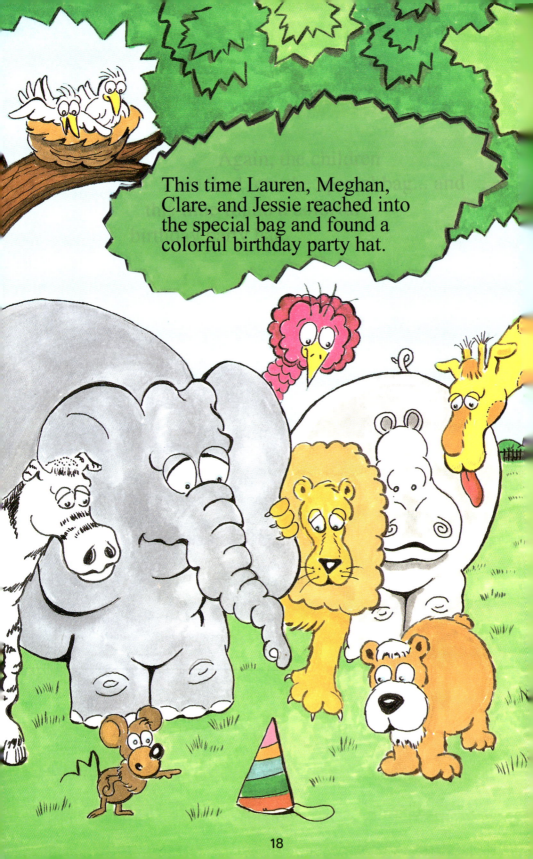

This time Lauren, Meghan, Clare, and Jessie reached into the special bag and found a colorful birthday party hat.

After slipping the hat over the rhino's nose, everyone could see it was a perfect fit. It was as fine as any horn could ever be. "Wow," cheered the rhino. "I was having a fit, but this is beautiful!" He was so pleased he gave a bouquet of very fine woven clover to everybody. He was blue no more.

"Oh boo hoo hoo, boo hoo hoo," everyone heard above. They had to use binoculars to see who was crying so way up high. On the top branch of a tall pine tree was a frightened stork. It appeared she might pine away, clinging to the branch with all her might. Around her were puffy blue clouds. She was crying so hard it made blue rain fall.

"I'm blue!" cried the stork. "I flew too high above the land, and now I'm afraid I'll land too hard!" There was nothing in the special bag that would help this situation. The only thing to do was to climb up there and help her down. But who would be the one to do it?

Lauren decided she would rescue the stork.

But when a dead limb snapped . . .

the little bear couldn't bear to look!

The ground was coming up fast when out of the blue and as quick as light, the stork swooped down to save the day. The landing was light and gentle beneath the tree.

The stork saved Lauren

"I saw you were in danger, so I lost all
my fear and flew down to rescue you. Now you are
safe and I'm blue no more!"

The zookeeper was rocking on a rock
with his head in his hands. "I'm blue
because the monkey hid my watch," he said. "I won't
know when it's feeding time without it.

The scraggly old monkey who wouldn't mind came to mind. He had taken the watch to a hollow log near by. Soon, everyone gathered there. I don't mind saying, it was a spooky place.

"Hiding the watch was mean," said
one child to the monkey.

After a moment, the monkey appeared. He didn't mean to act so mean. "I'm sorry," he said. "I took this watch and I know it was wrong. Now I'm blue and don't know what to do!"

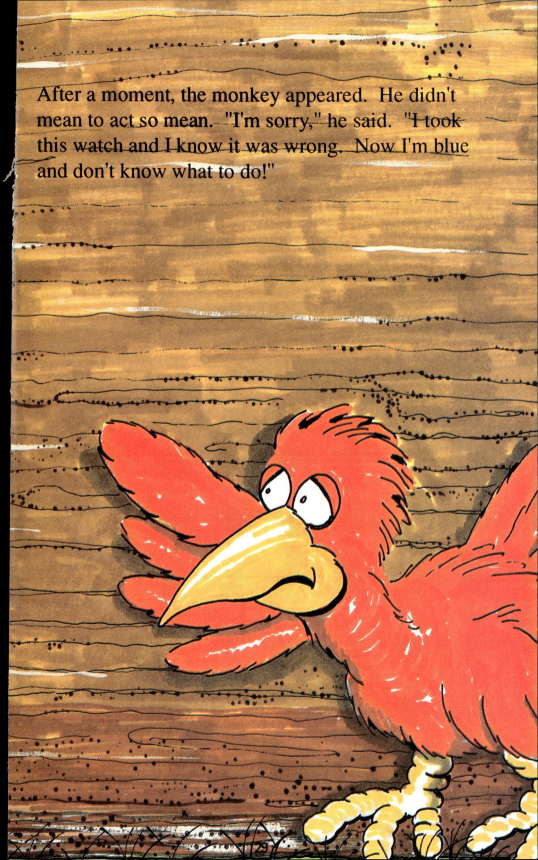

"I'm sure if we watch you return the watch, everyone will forgive you," said the zebra.

Then Lauren heard the rhino say, "And if you ask, maybe the zookeeper will help you find a nicer home."

So the monkey returned the pocketwatch, and Lauren exclaimed, "Now, all of the animals will be fed on time!" This made everyone happy.

At last the zoo was blue no more!

When all the children were ready to part, the animals did their part to say goodbye. "Horray, horray!" they all sang out. "You came to the zoo when we were blue, but now we're blue no more."

Cleveland Metroparks Zoo

BYE!

Come back soon Lauren!

ZOO

We'll All Miss You

Lauren

They sang and danced, and danced and sang, and the tall giraffe gave a ride to anyone who wanted. The zookeeper passed out balloons to all who went past.

There were red ones, green ones, yellow ones, and orange ones.... But no blue ones!

Here is the list of homonyms appearing throughout your story:

How many did you find?

page 7   pair-pear
page 9   red-read, ball-ball
page 10 gate-gait, long-longed, coat- (page 11 coat)
page 11 blue-blue, coat-(page 10 coat)
page 12 right-right, blue-blew
page 15 placed-place
page 17 faint-faint, to-two
page 19 fit-fit, fine-fine
page 20 hoo-who, pine-pine, might-might
page 21 land-land, to-too
page 22 bear-bear
page 24 light-light
page 26 rocking-rock
page 27 mind-mind
page 29 mean-mean
page 30 watch-watch
page 32 part-part
page 33 passed-past

Lauren